Helpin' Bugs

By Rosemary Lonborg

Illustrations by Diane R. Houghton

LITTLE FRIEND PRESS

SCITUATE, MASSACHUSETTS

Printed in the
United States of America

First U.S. edition 1995.
Published in the United States
in 1995 by Little Friend Press,
Scituate, Massachusetts.

ISBN 0-9641285-2-7

Library of Congress
Catalog Card Number: 95-077748

LITTLE FRIEND PRESS
28 NEW DRIFTWAY
SCITUATE, MASSACHUSETTS

For my niece, Hanna, with love
and
For my friends, Jenna and Matthew, with thanks.

Hanna felt sad.

Playing with toys
all by herself was
not fun at all.

"I wish I had
something to do,"
she sighed.

"Can I help you, Dad?" asked Hanna.

"Not right now, Hanna Banana," smiled Dad.
"I'm busy unpacking all these boxes.
Maybe you could help Mom."

"Can I help you, Mom?" asked Hanna.

"Not right now, Sweetie," said Mom.
"I have to feed the baby, but when
he takes his nap we can play together."

Hanna looked out the window
at all the other new houses.
She missed her old neighborhood
and her old friends.

"I wish I had someone to play with."

Then, Hanna watched curiously
as the garage door across
the street began to open.

And what she saw made her smile.

Down the stairs she flew...

"Mom, can I go outside?" asked
Hanna as she put on her coat.

"Where are you going, Hanna?"

"I think I see a friend to play with!
He lives across the street."

"Wait, Banana! I'll help you cross."

"Oh, Dad," laughed Hanna.
"I'm HANNA, just plain HANNA...
and I'm NOT a BANANA!"

The little boy across the street must certainly be important, she thought. He wore a big, red fireman's hat, and a shiny, gold sheriff's badge. He had big cowboy boots on his feet and a rope around his waist. He also wore a backpack that seemed to be filled with treasures.

Hi, I'm Hanna. What's your name?"

The little boy looked up at her and
answered "Douglas."

"What are you doing, Douglas?" asked Hanna.

"Helpin' bugs," he said.

Hanna had never seen anyone help a bug before.

"Well, do you want to help?"

"Sure!" said Hanna.

Finally, she could help someone!

Hanna and Douglas spent the afternoon
making their own bug village.

Douglas built a stick bridge for the bugs
to climb across the big crack in the sidewalk.

Hanna made a garden with yellow
dandelions and purple violets.

Cracker crumbs from
Douglas' backpack became
the Busy Bug Cafeteria.
Hanna watched the bugs
carry crumbs on their backs.

They made a bug hospital
with bug beds and a leaf hut
where bugs could find shade.

A path of grass led to…

a puddle where the bugs could
take a swim if they got hot.

Douglas used some acorn caps to
make a fleet of bug boats.

"What if bugs can't swim?" Hanna asked Douglas.
"Of course, bugs can swim, silly..." he said.
"Have you ever seen a drowning bug?"
"Well, I guess not," Hanna smiled.

Douglas knew an awful lot about bugs.

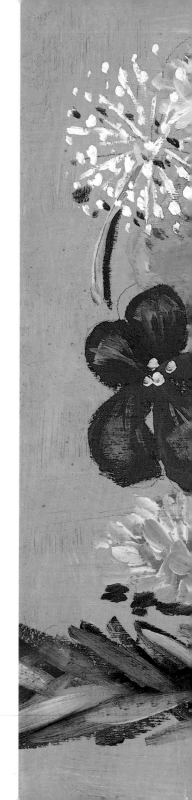

When they had
finished, they smiled...

and watched the
bugs climb happily
about their
wondrous surroundings.

Then Hanna heard her mother call, "H-A-N-N-A !"

"Oops! I have to go home now," Hanna jumped up.

"What will we do tomorrow, Douglas?"

"We'll help the bugs at your house."

Douglas smiled and waved good-bye.

At the dinner table that night,
Hanna told Mom and Dad all
about her new friend.

"Maybe you and Douglas would
like to play here tomorrow."

"That would be nice, Mom,"
Hanna said. "But we will
be much too busy to play."

"Busy? Doing what?"
Mom asked in surprise.

Hanna grinned and said, "Helpin' bugs!"